I stand with my tribe who have defined themselves through their continued support, and forever, for always, my reason, my Zu Zu.

The Amazing Zoe: A Queen Like Me

Copyright © 2020 Written by Valene Campbell, Illustrations by Arooba Bilal

For information about this title or to order other books and/or electronic media, please contact the publisher:

thezmh.com

Zou Zou Media House c/o Woolcock Patton, LLC

488 Schooley's Mountain Road, Bldg 1A

Hackettstown, NJ 07840

Printed in the United States of America

First Edition: September 2020

Publisher's Cataloging-in-Publication Data

Names: Campbell, Valene, author.

Title: The amazing Zoe : A Queen Like Me / Valene Campbell.

Description: Hackettstown, NJ : Woolcock Patton, 2020. | Includes 60 color illustrations. | Series: The Amazing Zoe's Adventures ; 2. | Audience: Ages 3-9. | Summary: Zoe and Kaitlyn love playing together; their favorite game is dress-up. One day, the girls decide to dress up as royals, but Kaitlyn refuses to let Zoe be the princess because she has not seen a princess like her before.

Identifiers: LCCN 2020913613 | ISBN 9781777189532 (hardback) | ISBN 9781777189549 (pbk.) | ISBN 9781777189556 (epub)

Subjects: LCSH: Friendship -- Juvenile literature. | Prejudices -- Juvenile fiction. | Princesses -- Juvenile fiction.| BISAC: JUVENILE FICTION / Diversity & Multicultural. | JUVENILE FICTION / Social Themes / Friendship. | JUVENILE FICTION / Social Themes / Prejudice & Racism.

Classification: LCC PZ7.1 C36 Qu4 2020 | [E]--dc22

LC record available at https://lccn.loc.gov/2020913613

The Amazing Zoe
A Queen Like Me!

Written by
Valene Campbell

Zoe thought of an idea as she almost finished cleaning her room. She said to herself, "Now that my room is clean,

I think I'll ask Mommy and Daddy if I can go out to play." She left her bedroom and went to see her mommy who was in the kitchen.

"Mommy, can I go over to Kaitlyn's house?" Zoe asked. "Sure, sweetheart, just make sure you're home before dinner.

We're making pizza tonight," Zoe's mommy said. "Ok, Mommy, see you soon!" Zoe said as she gathered a few toys.

Zoe couldn't wait to run through the door. She loved to visit her friend Kaitlyn who lived across the street.

They were the same age, went to the same school, and both loved to pretend and play dress up. They were best friends.

Zoe and Kaitlyn had many toys and costumes that they shared but there was one outfit that was extra special.

It was their absolute favourite! It was a princess outfit. It was a rose pink satin dress that was trimmed with pink lace. It had long laced sleeves and a collar that gently hugged the shoulders. The dress also had a long train that stretched almost halfway across the room. It was beautiful!

"I LOVE that dress!"

Zoe said, "Let's dress up as royals. Today, I'd like to be the princess."
"No way, I always play the princess, that's my part!" Kaitlyn demanded.
"But, it's my turn now!" Zoe said in anger.

When Kaitlyn put on the dress, Zoe felt like she didn't want to play anymore. Kaitlyn said to Zoe, "I don't know why you would want to play the princess anyway? They never look like you. They always look more like me?"

Zoe asked, "Why would you say that, princesses are girls and I'm a girl?!"

"Ya, but they always have hair and skin like me?" Kaitlyn said proudly.

"That isn't fair!" Zoe shouted.

Zoe began to cry, packed up her toys and said, "I'm going home!"

As Zoe dashed through the door, Kaitlyn's mother asked, "Wait, where are you going Zoe? You just got here."

Zoe didn't answer Kaitlyn's mother. She kept going and ran home.

When Zoe's mommy and daddy heard her coming through the door, they couldn't understand why she had come back so soon.

"Hi, Zoe, you're home early. Oh, no, are those tears I see? What happened?" Asked Zoe's mommy.

Zoe was so upset, she could hardly speak. She finally found the words and said, "Kaitlyn and I were playing dress-up and I wanted to play the princess this time.

I never get to wear the dress. Kaitlyn told me that I couldn't because princesses don't look like me."

Zoe's daddy replied, "Well, that's not true at all! There were hundreds of great kings, queens, princes and, yes, little princesses in Africa, where we are all originally from.

They all looked like you, me and Mommy."

Zoe's tears began to dry, she perked up and asked, "Really? Royalty in Africa? Like who?"
Come and sit down, we are going to share a few names of the queens with you, said Zoe's daddy.

Queen Amina [ah-mee-nuh] was the Queen of Zaria [zahr-ee-uh] Nigeria [nahy-jeer-ee-uh]. When she was a young girl, she was a Hausa [hou-sah] princess warrior from the Northwest region of Nigeria. She later became a queen.

Queen Nzinga [n-zin-ga] Mbandi [m-bahn-dee] was a strong leader of Angola [ang-goh-luh]. She had many kingdoms and fought hard for their freedom against the rule of the Portuguese [pawr-chuh-geez].

Queen Yaa Asantewa [ya-ah-san-tey-wah] reigned over the Ashanti [ah-shan-tee] Kingdom of Ghana. In 1900, she led a war against the British.

Queen Nandi [nahn-dee] was from the Zulu [zoo-loo] kingdom. She was the mother of Shaka [shaa-kuh], the greatest king the Zulus ever knew. Her advice led the Zulus to victory countless times.

Sylvia [sil-vee-uh] Nagginda [nah-gin-duh] is also known as the Nnabagereka [nah-bah-jer-kuh] which means wife of the current king. She is queen of the Kingdom of Buganda [boo-gan-duh], also known as modern-day Uganda [yoo-gan-duh]. The current queen is a charity worker for human rights, women's rights and the rights of children.

You see, there were many powerful rulers, kings and queens from many different countries and regions of Africa. Our black history as royals isn't spoken of because some people are filled with hate. They want to erase all memories of it. They don't want the rest of the world to hear our story. This is the unkindness of some of the past and present," Zoe's mommy explained.

We have to do our part by doing some of the homework ourselves. There are many books, and movies that can tell you all about African and African-American history," said Zoe's mommy.

Zoe couldn't believe all that she had learned from her parents. "Wow, Mommy, I didn't know all of this. I have to tell Kaitlyn. She better make me the princess next time," Zoe said with a frown.

"No sweetheart, not with anger. Kaitlyn didn't know about African royals because no one taught her. We can all go over to Kaitlyn's house tomorrow and speak to Kaitlyn and her parents," said Zoe's daddy.

Zoe started to feel a little bit better and said, "Ok, Daddy, I'd like that. Kaitlyn is still my friend, but I'm sad that she made me feel like I can't be a princess."

"My dear Zoe, you ARE a princess. Not just when you are playing dress up, but you are one every day. And when you grow up, my little princess will become a queen," Zoe's dad said with a smile. "Thank you Daddy," said Zoe as she smiled back.

"I'm ready to make pizza for my dinner. I'm hungry!"
Zoe said with excitement.

Zoe and her parents began to make their fresh, homemade pizza.

The next day, Zoe and her parents walked across the street for a welcomed visit to Kaitlyn and her family's house.

Zoe's dad had a big bag in his hand filled with a few special things.

Kaitlyn and her parents greeted Zoe and her parents at the door with some treats. They baked vanilla cupcakes with chocolate frosting and rainbow sprinkles on top.

They were Zoe and Kaitlyn's favourite flavour. Zoe was still angry about not being able to play the princess and said "NO!" to the cupcakes, then turned her head away. Kaitlyn became sad.

Zoe's mommy shared with Kaitlyn and Zoe the importance of sharing and taking turns when they play together. "It's about giving everyone an equal chance, " said Zoe's mommy.

family

Kaitlyn and her parents agreed but Zoe's parents had more to say. Zoe's parents shared that Ancient Africa had kings and queens who looked like them, who also ruled BIG kingdoms. They said some countries in Africa have royalty even now.

Kaitlyn and her family where surprised to hear about the kings and queens of Africa but were excited to learn more. Zoe's parents were happy to share many more stories.

Later that day, while all of the parents were still talking, Kaitlyn and Zoe skipped off to Kaitlyn's room where they usually played. Zoe brought the big bag that her dad had with her.

Kaitlyn said, "I'm sorry I've never let you play the princess Zoe. I've only seen princesses that look like me. I didn't know that ALL little girls can be princesses?"

"Yes, it's true Kaitlyn, ALL little girls can be princesses, but it's ok. I'm glad that you're my best friend." Said Zoe as they hugged.

"So what do you want to do now?" Kaitlyn asked.
"We can play dress up." Zoe grabbed her big brown
bag and looked inside.

Zoe took out a beautiful, soft purple and green dress and a tall crown from the bag. The crown had red and green shiny jewels on the front.

"WHOA, that's so pretty. What is that?" Kaitlyn asked. "Can I touch it?" She was very curious.

"Sure. Daddy picked it up for me yesterday. I think it's my new favourite outfit." Zoe began to put on the dress and Kaitlyn helped while standing behind. Zoe and Kaitlyn smiled. They were both amazed by the beauty.

"Is that a princess outfit?" Kaitlyn asked.

"No, it isn't a princess outfit," said Zoe standing tall and strong. "It's my Nnabagereka [nah-bah-jer-kuh] outfit. Today, I'm playing Queen Sylvia of Buganda, who is a queen like me!"

Zoe invited Kaitlyn to put on her princess outfit and said, " When daddy picked up my outfit, he got something for you too." Zoe took a beautiful beaded necklace out of the brown paper bag and gave it to Kaitlyn. "Here you go, now you have a piece of Africa with you too," Zoe said cheerfully.

"Cheers"

Kaitlyn was so happy, she placed the necklace around her neck right away. Then they sat down together, as best friends, for an afternoon tea party to end the day.

MESSAGE FROM THE AUTHOR,

Thank you for reading the Amazing Zoe, I hope you enjoyed the story. Just as Zoe and Kaitlyn were able to learn more about each other through history books, I encourage you to also continue reading and discovering the untold stories of people and places of the world. Please see the list of references and suggested readings below:

REFERENCES

1) Onyeakagbu, Adaobi. "Ancient African Queens Everyone Should Know About." www.Pulse.ng, 23 August 2018, https://www.pulse.ng/lifestyle/food-travel/people-and-culture-ancient-african-queens-everyone-should-know-about/esk5qqq

2) Schwartz-Bart, Simone. In Praise of Black Women, Volume 1: Ancient African Queens. University of Wisconsin Press, October 1, 2001.

3) Nnabagereka of Buganda. (2020, July 30). In Wikipedia. Retrieved from URLhttps://en.wikipedia.org/wiki/Nnabagereka_of_Buganda

SUGGESTED READINGS

1) Schweitzer, Richard. iAfrica: Ancient History Untold. Forbidden Fruit Books LLC. November 9th 2013.

2) Commey, Pusch Komiete. 7 Amazing African Queen and Dynasties, Volume 1. CreateSpace Independent Publishing Platform; 1 edition June 4, 2018.